THE
TALENT SHOW
FROM THE
BLACK LAGOON

THE
TALENT SHOW
FROM THE
BLACK LAGOON

by Mike Thaler
Illustrated by Jared Lee

SCHOLASTIC INC.
New York   Toronto   London   Auckland   Sydney
Mexico City   New Delhi   Hong Kong   Buenos Aires

To Alan Boyko,
My FAIR-haired friend
—M.T.

To Mom, who always reminded her young son
that his talent was a gift from God.
—J.L.

ISBN-13: 978-0-439-43894-0
ISBN-10: 0-439-43894-2

Text copyright © 2003 by Mike Thaler.
Illustrations copyright © 2003 by Jared D. Lee Studio, Inc.

48 47 46 45 44 43 42 41   17 18 19 20

Printed in the U.S.A.   40
First printing, January 2003

CONTENTS

CLAP CLAP
CLAP

CHAPTER 1
THE SHOW *MUST* GO ON

We're having a talent show. I've heard all about them. Ten hours of endless embarrassment and nonstop nausea. And that's just for the audience.

But it's a lot worse for the performers! Some people never recover their shattered egos.

But Mrs. Green says every one of us has to do something. She says we must be onstage for at least a minute, and not longer than an hour. I *really* want to be on the stage . . . yeah, the *first stage* out of town.

CHAPTER 2
SHOW BUZZ

On our way home, I ask my pals what they're going to do. Eric says that he's going to tell jokes. He'll be some sort of a stand-up *comic-kazi*. I'm sure we've heard all his jokes already.

Freddy says he's going to recite his recipe for apple turnovers. Derek is going to spin a hula hoop. Randy will perform his most mystifying magic trick. He's going to pull his head out of a hat!

Penny is excited to lip-sync Beethoven's 9th Symphony!

And Doris, who takes ballet lessons, says she's going to dance the dying swan from *Swine Luck*—or something like that.

Everyone asks me what I'm going to do. I just stare out the foggy window and mumble, "You'll see."

CHAPTER 3
STAR BRIGHT

What am I going to do?

My major talents are very specialized. I'm a great burper. I can burp "Yankee Doodle" after drinking a soda.

I can wiggle my ears and cross my eyes at the same time. I can touch the tip of my nose with the end of my tongue. But Freddy can pick his nose!

I can squirt milk out of my nose. I did at Thanksgiving, but no one applauded.

I can make my armpits quack like a duck.

QUACK

QUACK

QUACK

QUACK

I can stand upside down if someone holds my feet. Or I can stand right side up if there's a floor.

I can tie my body in a knot. But it takes an hour to get it untied!

I can make a *pigzilla* monster face! Or do my Count Dracula imitation!

I can blow in a bottle and sound like a foghorn.

PLUMMP
PLUMMP
PLUMMP

I just don't know what to do . . . I have so many talents.

CHAPTER 4
MOTHER KNOWS BEST

I share my problem with my mom. BIG MISTAKE! She decides to help me.

She suggests that I do a nice little dance. NEVER! Then she says I have a sweet singing voice. FORGET IT! Next, she tells me that I have a nice smile. Couldn't I just smile for a minute? I DON'T THINK SO!

Now she really puts on her thinking cap. I'm in big trouble! "I know," she says. "You can learn how to play the piano." And before I can throw up or even yell, she's already calling Mrs. Fumble, the piano teacher. Oh, great, now I have to take piano lessons!

FANTASTIC!

CHAPTER 5
TREBLE TROUBLE

The first lesson is a complete disaster. I have two left hands and they're all thumbs. I finally find the middle C and hit it with my elbow.

Mrs. Fumble wears tons of perfume. She smells like a flower show. I will smell like a wedding for a week.

She's as big as a wrestler and always sits on the little piano bench with me. I can hardly see around her. And my side of the bench keeps lifting up in the air. She asks me why I want to play the piano. I say, "I don't. I'd rather be playing baseball."

29

My mom says that one day I will be the hit of the party when I sit down to play. I don't want to be the hit of the party. I just want to get through one minute onstage.

CHAPTER 6
KEY BORED

Instead of playing baseball, building race-car models, or going swimming and becoming a swordfish . . . here I am still practicing. This is hard.

I have to play the same thing
over and over for a whole hour.
And what makes things worse—
I have to listen to it.

The only good thing about playing the piano is that you can do it sitting down. After four weeks, five lessons, and thousands of hours of practicing, I can now play "Chopsticks." The good news is it takes just about a minute to play.

33

CHAPTER 7

SHOW BIZ GOSSIP

I call all the other kids to hear how they're doing. Eric tells me all his jokes. I've heard them before. And they're about as funny as a math test.

Freddy shares his recipe for apple turnovers. It sounds like the only thing it will turn over is your stomach.

Derek says he's a little bit dizzy from all the hula-hooping. Randy the Magnificent tells me that great magicians never give away their tricks.

Penny says her lips are in a cast. She sprained them practicing. And Doris asks me if I have any feathers for her costume.

This is going to be quite a show.
I can see it now . . .

CHAPTER 8
STAGE STRUCK OUT

The auditorium lights dim. The spotlight falls on Eric. But it doesn't hurt him. He gets up and tells his first joke. No one laughs. He tries a second joke. Again, no one laughs. Here comes his third joke. It's about the principal. Everyone laughs and he gets sent to the principal's office.

Then a hush falls over the audience. Freddy, who's wearing a chef's hat, opens his cookbook and reads the recipe for apple turnovers. Everyone's mouth is watering. It's close to lunchtime.

40

Then Randy comes out. He's wearing a magician's hat. He tells the audience that he's going to pull a human head out of it. There's a slow drumroll. And he pulls the hat off his head, bows, and walks quickly off the stage. Everyone is mystified!

Now Derek comes out. He's wearing a hula hoop. He spins it once and it spirals down to his feet. Everyone boos. He lifts up the hula hoop and tries again. It drops straight to the floor. But Derek doesn't give up. He keeps trying for an hour. Finally, Mrs. Green comes out and pulls him off the stage with the hoop.

BOO

BOO

BOO

43

Penny walks onstage. Her lips are out of the cast. Soon, the CD is playing, and we have to wait four movements until people start singing. But when they finally do, the CD starts skipping. Penny starts to cry and skips offstage. I hope there's not a talent scout in the audience.

MY LOVE IS
MY LOVE IS
MY LOVE IS

The lights on the stage turn blue, and Doris comes out covered in feathers. She spins around, but her feathers begin to fly off and float over the audience.

Dying Swan is right. When she's done, she's ready for the oven.

Then it's my turn. Mr. Smudge, the school janitor, rolls out a concert grand piano. I come out and bow politely. I sit down at the keyboard and lift my hands. My two fingers are poised in the air. Suddenly, everyone begins sniffing and holding their noses. The entire auditorium is filled with the scent of lilacs—shades of Mrs. Fumble.

46

Soon, everyone runs outside to get a breath of fresh air. I'm sitting at the piano alone—all that practicing for nothing.

Suddenly, I wake up. It's time for bed. I can't believe the talent show's tomorrow.

CHAPTER 9
IT'S CURTAINS

That night, I have a dream. Well, more like a nightmare.

There's a bright stage and millions of people are sitting out in the audience. I'm standing in the middle of the stage. I can hear them all breathing. I'm wearing a purple tuxedo with a silver bow tie.

I take off my pink top hat. I announce that I will pull a live rabbit out of my top hat. There's a slow drumroll as I reach into the hat and pull out a mouse. Everyone shouts, "That's not a rabbit!"

I reach back in the hat and pull out a cat. The audience yells, "That's not a rabbit, either!"

BOO

I keep on trying the trick until the stage looks like Noah's Ark. Everything from aardvarks to zebras—but not one rabbit. Everyone boos and then throws carrots at me. And finally, the curtain comes down.

BOO

BOO

BOO

BOO

CHAPTER 10
A STAR IS BORN

Well, it's ten A.M. Showtime!

Everyone in school fills the auditorium. Little kids, big kids, teachers, and relatives—all expecting to be entertained. We huddle together backstage. Doris is in her feathers. Freddy is in his chef's hat. Penny is wearing lipstick. Randy is in his magician's hat. And Eric is wearing a red ball on his nose. That's funny stuff!

The lights slowly dim, the curtain rises, and we point to Eric. He's first. He steps out on the stage. All eyes are on him. He taps the microphone. It sounds like elephants on a giant trampoline.

He clears his throat and tells his first joke. Everyone laughs.

CLAP CLAP
CLAP

They applaud when Freddy reads his recipe. And they gasp when Randy takes off his hat and pulls out Waldo, our class hamster.

Derek has tied his hoop to his belt. And he spins around!

CLAP

CLAP
CLAP

CLAP

Penny lip-syncs "Girls Just Wanna Have Fun." And everyone in the audience wants to have fun, too!

CLAP
CLAP
CLAP

Doris gets through her dance, only losing three feathers. That's certainly a feather in her cap.

Mr. Smudge slowly rolls out the piano. I come out and sit down. Then I take off my shoes and my socks.

CLAP CLAP   Bravo Bravo

I play "Chopsticks" like it's never been played before . . . with my toes! And the audience goes wild.

CLAP CLAP

CLAP CLAP

62

We're a hit! I have snatched
victory from the *toes of defeat*.

This is my first step to stardom. I hope we can have another talent show next week. I will play "Chopsticks" with my elbows. I am just getting warmed up.